GLASS AND SASS

AN AMETHYST'S WAND SHOP MYSTERIES PREQUEL

LAURA GREENWOOD

ARIZONA TAPE

© 2021 Laura Greenwood & Arizona Tape

All rights reserved. This book or parts thereof may not be reproduced in any form, stored in any retrieval system, or transmitted in any form by any means – electronic, mechanical, photocopy, recording or otherwise – without prior written permission of the published, except as provided by United States of America copyright law. For permission requests, write to the publisher at "Attention: Permissions Coordinator," at the email address; lauragreenwood@authorlauragreenwood.co.uk.

Visit Laura Greenwood's website at:

www.authorlauragreenwood.co.uk

Visit Arizona Tape's website at:

www.arizonatape.com

Cover by Vampari Designs

Glass and Sass is a work of fiction. Names, characters, places, and incidents are the products of the author's imagination or are used fictitiously. Any resemblance to actual persons, living or dead, businesses, companies, events, or locales is entirely coincidental.

❦ Created with Vellum

BLURB

Amethyst likes to do things her own way, even when that means being suspended by the Centre for Wand Control when she uses a material she shouldn't when making wands, ending up with her Grammie's wand making license being suspended.

Amy is determined to put it right, even if she has to go toe to toe with the CWC and prove that sea glass isn't an unstable component of wands.

Can she get the suspension lifted?

-

Glass and Sass is prequel to the Amethyst's Wand Shop Mysteries series. The series is urban fantasy mystery with an underlying slow burn romance, the prequel focuses on Amy's first clash with the Centre for Wand Control.

CHAPTER ONE

I sip my tea as I make my way down the street. People haven't started emerging from their homes yet and if I had my way, I wouldn't have either. I'd be wrapped up in my blankets and dozing away still. But Grammie says there's no rest when it comes to wand making. Too little time, too many wands. And who was I to dispute that?

"No rest for the witches," I mutter to myself. I laugh softly, wishing someone could've heard my excellent joke. Then again, maybe not.

People aren't exactly friendly this early. Or ever, really. Especially not to those of us who work in retail.

The little bell above the door tinkles happily as I step into the family Wand Shop. "Morning."

From behind the counter, Grammie shoots me one of her signature warm smiles. "Morning, Amy. You're bright and early. Except you don't look too bright and..." She checks her watch. "You're not early either."

"It's before nine," I mutter under my breath, not intending for her to actually hear me.

The look on Grammie's face says it all.

Oops. My bad.

"It's just as well you're here," she muses. "We have a full client list today. Including the Harringtons and their delightful daughter."

I groan. "Please tell me you're joking?" Cecilia used to be in my class at school, and she wasn't someone I was eager to spend any more time with than necessary. That girl is a witch with a capital b.

"They're good customers of ours."

"You only say that because they pay well," I point out.

Grammie chuckles. "When this shop is yours, you'll learn that is exactly what it takes for a client to be a good one."

"When this shop is mine, blablabla," I mock. "I told you, Topaz is your girl."

"No offence to your sister, but she'll run this Wand Shop when hell freezes over."

I know how attached she is to the shop and while I enjoy wand making, it isn't my passion like hers.

Carefully, I approach the counter and shoot Grammie an appeasing smile. "Grammie… I know you love the shop, but it's just not my dream. I want to join the Paranormal Police Department and you know my application is pending."

"About that…" She sighs as she pulls the latex gloves off with a snap. "There's something we need to talk about."

"My letter came, didn't it?" I ask. Trying to temper my excitement over my dreams coming true, I take another sip of my tea.

Ouch. Why is it so hot? The little warning they put on the label should be bigger.

"It did," Grammie says.

"And?"

"You should sit down, Amy," she repeats.

"Okay…" I move deeper into the shop, making sure to pat the stone cat on the head as I pass. It's unforgivable to ignore Herbert.

I scrape the chair back, wincing at the screech. I could lift it, but I'm too committed to the movement.

Grammie winces but doesn't say anything.

"All right, lay it on me," I say.

"A letter came…"

My heart pounds in my chest. A letter is a good thing, right? Or maybe not. Getting one could mean acceptance into magic schools, but it could also mean being summoned to the gyno. The latter definitely doesn't count in the fun column of anyone sane.

"What does it say?" I ask when she doesn't continue. That isn't a good sign. Or is it?

"Just remember, I'm here for whatever you need," Grammie assures me.

"Are you just saying that so I remember to visit you from the PPD Academy?" I ask.

Grammie's solemn face crushes the glimmer of hope and I frown.

"Is it not from the PPD?" That's the only reason I can think of for the way she's acting. She knows how crushed I'll be if they don't take me.

"It is, but..." She pulls a letter from one of the many drawers and holds it out to me. "It's not good news, Amy."

I accept the crumpled piece of paper and scan it quickly, desperate to know what it's all about. "They rejected my application? What? Why!"

"It doesn't say."

"I. But... I don't understand..." I flip the letter, hoping for an explanation on the backside, but there isn't one. Just an elegant signature signing off and wishing me well in my future endeavours. Assholes.

Grammie places a hand on my shoulder. "I'm sorry, dear."

"Fuck them."

"Language."

"Curse them."

"Much better." With a saddened smile, she reaches back into the drawer. "There's something else…"

"It can't get much worse," I mutter, my mouth ashen.

"Well… That wasn't the only letter that arrived this morning."

While Grammie had sounded deflated when she handed me my PPD letter, she sounds downright devastated now.

That isn't good news.

I swallow a lump away. "What is it? Is it Mum? Dad? Topaz?"

"No, it's the shop." She hands me the second letter. "The Centre of Wand Control has temporarily suspended my license."

"What?!"

I bounce up from the chair, my sadness erased by

the bubbling anger. Nobody messes with my Grammie's shop, not even the CWC.

My eyes tear through the letter, scanning the passages in the hope that their message would change. Why are they suspending our shop's license?

"Unauthorised wand making on the premises?" I read out loud. "Are they serious?"

"The CWC is always serious," Grammie replies. "They're launching an investigation and in the meantime, we're reduced to repairs and maintenance."

"I don't understand. How can they think that you're doing something wrong? You? You're always teaching me the rules, blabbering on and on about what is and isn't allowed. You probably know the rulebook better than whoever wrote it!"

"I do not blabber, Amethyst."

Oh no. That tone of voice is never a good one. I know I'm in trouble when Grammie uses it.

"I'm sorry, that's not what I meant," I correct myself instantly. "I know what you're telling me is important."

She sighs. "But you don't want to be a wandmaker."

"I…" There are no words to describe the complexity of how I feel about our profession.

It isn't that I didn't like making wands. Far from it. I love the feel of wood beneath my hands, and the way different things can make it more powerful. But it's not my primary calling. Wand making is a family business, and I don't want to simply disappear into the long line of makers without being myself first.

Hence the PPD. It would be awesome to spend time solving crimes and keeping the paranormal community safe. The sting is made worse by the fact they keep advertising that they wanted witches and mages to sign up because of our unique skill sets.

I close my eyes and take a deep breath, trying not to let myself shout out about the unfairness of it all.

"I'm sorry, Amy," Grammie says. "You can try again next year?" she suggests softly.

I shake my head, choosing to ignore the single tear rolling down my cheek. "It's not that," I counter. "I know I can try again with the PPD. I'm more worried about the CWC and why they think this is acceptable. I'm going to get to the bottom of this. I promise."

She smiles at me dotingly. She probably doesn't think I have a chance at doing that. The CWC is secretive at the best of times. I don't want to think about how they are at the worst of times and this surely is the worst of times.

With a sigh, I rise from the chair and tighten my jacket. "I'll let you deal with the Harringtons. I'm going to have a talk with the CWC."

"Be careful, Amy." Grammie moves to make eye contact with Herbert. "Make sure she's safe, will you?"

"I'll be safe," I tell both Grammie and the stone cat. "Don't worry about me, Herb."

The stone cat vibes reassuringly and I take that as encouragement.

With a nod, I leave the wand shop, ready to launch my own investigation and make the CWC regret ever messing with my family.

Luckily, I know just where to start.

CHAPTER TWO

I DROP my empty takeaway cup into a bin as I approach the corner of the street that has the unfortunate job of housing the local Centre for Wand Control office. It's far from the biggest in the country, but it's likely to be the one that's investigating us.

And it's the only one within easy walking distance of our shop.

The building looms above me, grey and uninviting. Why do they have to have such a boring looking building? It's like they don't want visitors. I know that if I ask I'll get the standard response that they're trying to put humans off going inside, but that's ridiculous and like they haven't heard of a little thing called spell casting. A little bit of that and any potential human problems go away.

Oh well. It won't matter how boring the outside is when I have to go in. I hope they at least have comfortable seats in the waiting room.

I stride forward, projecting as much confidence as I can. Perhaps they will simply tell me what I need to know, and I won't have to do too much work to uncover it. A small part of me would be disappointed in the lack of challenge. All right. A large part of me.

The automatic doors part the moment I stand in front of them. Perhaps we should put something similar into the shop? No, that's not a good idea. Herbert would probably take it upon himself to open them and set off the bell every time my back was turned just to drive me crazy. To be honest, I'm surprised he doesn't do something similar to that already. He's a very mischievous sort of gargoyle. Most of them are far more serious than he is. Not that I'm complaining. Life would be dull without Herb.

The witch behind the front desk looks up from examining her bright red nails. I don't understand how she could work with wands with such long fake nails, they strike me as incredibly impractical.

Despite that, I find myself a little self-conscious

about my own neatly trimmed short nails and have to resist the urge to hide them behind my back.

"Do you have an appointment?" she asks flatly, barely giving me a second glance.

I roll my eyes. So much for British hospitality. Hasn't she heard of customer service?

"I was looking to speak to Mr Richards," I say, assuming the man who signed the letter about the investigation is the person I need to talk to. I'm well aware that it's probably a premade letter with the signature just copied in, but even if someone else put his name on it, he should be willing to back it up.

If not, then I'll make it so he does.

"He only takes appointments," she responds in a bored tone.

"Then I'd like to make an appointment with him," I say through gritted teeth. It's so typical. The CWC always wants other people to do things on their terms, but they aren't interested in working around other people's. I have a few choice words for upper management about that.

If I ever get in front of them.

She turns away from me and types something into her computer. "When did you have in mind?"

"I'm free now." I leave off the obviously even though I want to say it.

"The earliest slot available is in three weeks," the secretary chimes lifelessly.

"Three weeks?" The investigation is next weekend, three weeks isn't going to cut it. "But I need to see him now."

"Unfortunately, he only takes appointments. Mr Richards is a very busy man."

I try to stop myself from rolling my eyes. This woman is just doing her job and it isn't fair of me to take my frustration on Mr Richards out on her when all she's doing is repeating the line he probably tells her to say to every unhappy wandmaker who ends up through the CWC's door.

Which is probably a lot. They're known for being rather heavy-handed when they want to be.

Frustrated, I draw in a clenched breath. "It's really urgent and it won't take long. Is there no way to get in earlier?"

She shoots me an apologetic smile, the first hint that she's not happy with having to deny me as much as she is. "I'm sorry, he only—"

"Takes appointments," I finish her sentence for her. "It's fine, I'll find another way."

With the disappointment coursing through me, I turn away from the front desk. Clearly, the customer isn't king here.

Maybe I can't get an appointment, but Mr Richards has to come and go and, lucky for me, there's a nice lounge right near the entrance of the building. It seems like the drab and boringness is exclusive to the outside of the building. The red cushions looked a little uncomfortable, but there's a vending machine with cold drinks and snacks. Enough to keep me going while I camp out and wait for him to come down.

I smile at the receptionist, but she's already turned back to her nails. Instead of engaging with her again, I make my way over to the machines, and grab myself a can of lemonade and a chocolate bar. It's the kind of breakfast Grammie would take one look at and tut. She'd never say anything other than that, but her expression alone would be enough to have me reaching for a healthier option.

It's a good job she isn't here right now.

Besides, if I'm going to have to take on the bureaucracy of the CWC, then I'm going to do it with tasty snacks. That's why I always keep some in my bag.

I sit back down, ignoring the pointed looks from the woman behind the desk who seems to have noticed that I haven't disappeared. It's safe to say she doesn't like me. Probably because I want her to do her job. Some people are funny like that.

My mind begins to wander. Is Grammie doing okay back at the shop? Have the Harringtons arrived already? I hope she isn't too stressed without me there. Then again, with the ban on making wands, she doesn't really need me. Especially as she's been running the shop on her own for a long time until she started training me to take over at fifteen. I've never asked her why Mum or one of my Aunts didn't take over.

I reach to my waist to touch my wand to make sure it's still there. I do that every so often when I'm in public to make sure no one has taken it. Wand theft is more common than witches like to admit and comes with more paperwork than I care to fill out at this time in the morning. Despite each wand being the perfect match for its owner, they'll still work for any witch. Unlike mage staffs that'll only work for the mage who crafted it. I envy them that. I hate it when people ask to borrow my wand and wish I could say no.

With nothing else to do, I pull out my phone to play a game. The screen flashes with colour and with deft fingers, I match tiles and symbols. If I were in the mood to lie to myself, I'd say this was my way of keeping my mind sharp. In reality, it's a way to stop me getting so bored that I do something stupid. It has happened before. More than once. And it almost never ends well.

CHAPTER THREE

It isn't until I've waited for about fifteen minutes that I realise I don't know what Mr Richards looks like. I just saw the name on the CWC letter we received. It's a bit of a hiccup in my plan to accost him.

This is why people think things through before doing them. I need to learn to do that.

I scrunch the wrapper of my chocolate bar into a ball and aim for the bin.

Score!

A small victory, but one I'm going to take at this point.

The ding of an elevator calls my attention away from my sporting proficiency. Someone is coming.

Hopefully Mr Richards, I forgot to charge my phone last night so can't play games for too long.

A short man in a suit strides across the entrance hall. I have no idea if he's the man I'm looking for, but he's the right gender, which is a start.

I jump to my feet, only wondering if I have chocolate stains on my shirt when I'm already halfway across the room. Oh well, too late now.

"Hi," I chirp, popping up in front of him so he has no chance but to engage and can't just walk away.

He gives me a startled look from over his thin glasses. "Yes?"

"Are you Mr Richards?" I ask.

"No, sorry." He pushes past me.

As he walks away, I address another man who seems to have appeared. It must be break time, because there are now several people coming from the elevators.

"Hi. Are you Mr Richards?"

The slender man shakes his head as he walks past me.

Damn it.

I don't know how many people I question before the receptionist waves me to her desk. Finally.

Hello," I grin. "Can I see Mr Richards now?"

She sighs dramatically. "I told you, he's only available for appointments."

"Then why did you call me?"

"To ask you to leave. You're bothering people.

"I'm not bothering anyone," I deny. "It's not forbidden to talk to people, is it?"

The secretary glares at me as she taps her long nails on her desk. "No, it's not. But—"

"Sorry, got to go. Saw someone that might be Mr Richards," I interrupt, rushing away to the latest man that arrived. It's unlikely that he's going to be who I'm looking for, but if I don't ask, it'll definitely be him.

Before I can talk to the other man, the secretary calls me back yet again.

"Wait!" She sighs dramatically and shakes her head like I'm giving her the worst headache. Maybe I have. It wouldn't be the first time either.

I pause. "I'm listening."

"I'll give Mr Richards a call to see if he might have five minutes, but if he's not available, will you please go away and make an appointment in a few weeks?" she asks.

"Deal." Who says you can't annoy the big companies into doing what you want them to? It's not my preferred method of getting things done, but it isn't my fault they've made their staff hard to make appointments with.

She picks up her old-fashioned phone and punches in a couple of numbers. She shoots me an exhausted smile as she waits and bobs her head up and down.

"Ah, Richard. I have a young lady here that's desperate for a moment of your time… No, she's not scheduled in, she just showed up. Yes, I told her you only take appointments… I don't know what she wants." She muffles the speaker part of her phone and glares at me. "What do you want?"

I hold out the letter that arrived at the shop earlier today. "Suspended license."

The woman groans. "Suspended license. I know… Thank you." She clicks the phone down and sighs. "You're in luck, Mr Richards has agreed to see you. Fifth floor, turn to the right and the second office on the left."

"Great! Thank you." I shoot her a dazzling smile. "Oh, and the candy bars in your vending machine are delightful."

She shakes her head but seems glad to be rid of me. I don't blame her. If anyone has any complaints about the ways I've accosted them, it's probably her who will have to deal with them.

I try to ignore the kernel of guilt growing within me. I don't want to make anyone's job harder, even if that's what the CWC is doing to Grammie and I can't ignore that, especially when they haven't given an adequate reason for why they're doing this to her.

I make my way over to the elevator, touching my wand to make sure it hasn't disappeared since I last checked on it. Unsurprisingly, it's still there and still safe. One of these days I'll start trusting it isn't going to run off.

A small snort escapes me.

The day I stop checking on my wand is the day it does go missing. And I'm not going to let that happen. I'd be lost without it. Not because I can't do things without magic, I have plenty of experience on that front. But because magic and my wand are such important parts of me. I can't imagine not having that connection to who I am any more.

A shiver runs down my spine at the thought.

"Pull yourself together, Amy," I mutter as I step into the elevator, drawing a funny look from the woman already inside.

I ignore her. It's better that way.

The elevator brings me to the fifth floor and I skip through the boring grey halls. Most of the offices have some kind of thin window next to the door and I can't help sneak a peek inside. Round tables with people in suits, projectors and whiteboards with boring charts, and all kinds of paperwork. I've never seen anything so boring in my life.

Glad I don't spend my time behind a desk, I turn towards the left and search for the right office. Luckily there are gold signs on the doors.

There.

Richard Richards.

Oh, poor man. No wonder he's so cranky. I would be if my name was Amethyst Amethysts. Not that witches really have surnames. Normally we just use our coven name if we need one. Though it seems this witch has gone in a bit of a different direction. I bet he's regretting it now.

I knock thrice and wait politely to be called in. Contrary to what Grammie says and the secretary probably thinks, I do have manners.

"Come in!" a low voice calls.

Ah, good. He's not going to pretend he isn't expecting me. Things are definitely picking up for Team Amy.

CHAPTER FOUR

A MAN with long grey hair and stern glasses glares at me from behind his massive desk. He folds his hands and sighs. "So what I can do for you, Miss…"

"Amethyst of the Gemstone Coven," I answer, hoping he isn't going to use my coven name to refer to me the entire time. It's annoying and doesn't feel like me. "You suspended the license for my Grammie's shop and I want to know why."

He looks a little taken aback. Maybe he isn't used to people wanting to know why the CWC makes some of its decisions. "Pardon?"

"You suspended our license but it doesn't say why. Doesn't matter, it's bullshit anyway. Grammie would never do anything wrong. Never. She's the most honest, hard-working witch there is. Our wands are up to standard and freaking awesome." I cross my arms and give him a look that dares him to contradict what I'm saying.

"Miss Gemstone, if you don't agree with the suspension, you can lodge a request for a revision."

Ugh. Bureaucracy. What's the point of it when it all takes so long?

"So if I do that, does that mean we can keep operating in the meantime?" I ask.

"No, until we've reviewed the case again, I'm afraid the suspension remains."

I narrow my eyes at him. "And how long will that take?"

Mr Richard glances at his watch. "Two to six weeks. Now, if you don't mind, I have an appointment in—"

"I do mind. Can you at least tell me why our license was suspended?"

"Miss Gemstone, I don't personally work the cases. I'm the head of the department."

I show him the letter. "This is your signature, isn't it?"

"I… It is."

"You signed off on the suspension, so you must know why."

An awkward silence hangs in the office as he casts his eyes down. "It's pre-printed."

"Pre-printed?" I scoff even though I already suspected as much. "That's even worse. So you pre-signed off on something and you don't even know what?"

"Listen, Miss Gemstone, I appreciate what you're doing, but I really have to—"

"No! I want to know why we got suspended and how we can fix it."

Maybe it's stupid to barge in uninvited or to shout at this important man from the CWC, maybe I'm making things worse, but I can't just sit and do nothing. This is my Grammie's life's work. If she can't make wands… I don't know what she'd do. She isn't the type to go sit on some beach and sip mai-tais. Her face is under the term workaholic in the dictionary.

Mr Richards hesitates for a couple of seconds before he groans. "If I check your file, will you get out of my office?"

I beam. "Yes." That's all I wanted in the first place. Though maybe it isn't a good thing if I end up learning that if I keep pushing people, I'll get what I want.

"Great." He pushes his glasses further up his nose

and hovers his fingers over his keyboard. Click, click, click, letter per letter. He types painstakingly slowly. I hope he isn't doing it on purpose. Though if he isn't, I have to wonder how this man is the head of the department?

After what feels like an eternity, he nods. "Ah, here. Gemstone Coven. Amethyst's Wand Shop."

"That's the one."

"Suspended for… usage of an unlicensed magnifier," he says, looking away from the screen and back to me.

"What!?" I lunge forward to look at his computer, but he shields his screen and glares at me.

Right, privacy. And boundaries. I need to remember to respect them.

He waits for me to sit down before he resumes talking. "A report was filed about a wand with unlicensed material registered from your shop. We assessed the remnant traces of the magic and verified the foreign nature of the magnifier."

"Who filed the report?" I ball my hands into fists. "It better not be the snooty Harringtons. They lied about the wand we made for their daughter and called it defective just to get a free upgrade and that's not the first time they've pulled that stunt. I swear, if it's them, I will knock them off their brooms the next time—"

"The report came from the PPD," he cuts me off, his tone revealing that he's more than a little fed up with me right now.

Shit.

I reach down to touch my leg where my wand is tucked away in the custom sleeve. I completely forgot they tested it when I applied to the police force. They must have detected the unregistered sea glass that forgot I put it in.

Fuck.

Grammie's shop is in the weeds and it's... my fault? I did this...?

I pull my wand out and stare at it, trying to make sense of everything but not managing to fully process it.

"Listen, I can explain," I insist, trying not to let panic take over. I place my wand on the desk. "My Grammie has been teaching me how to make wands and I've been experimenting with the craft, but it's not my dream. You see, I applied to the PPD and used this wand which happens to have a little bit of sea glass in it. Now before you say it, yes, I know sea glass is technically an unregistered magnifier but I used it as a sentimental component. That's allowed, right?"

Mr Richards' expression remains unchanged. "Miss Gemstone, I'm sorry to say but there's really nothing I can do for you. You should file for a reassessment or wait for the inspection to clear things up."

"But—"

"In fact, I'm obligated to write up your confession and add it to your file."

My heart sinks. "What? What confession?"

"That you're indeed using unregistered materials."

"Hold up! No, I said I used a little bit of sea glass in my personal wand. Personal. It has nothing to do with the shop or Grammie. Besides, it's a sentimental component. I found this piece of glass on the beach when I was young. The core magnifier of my wand is an amethyst gem," I protest. How is this happening?

The man across me adjusts his glasses. "Unregistered magnifiers are dangerous and unpredictable. That's why they're unlicensed."

I know he's just quoting the rules, and that they're there for a reason, but it's still frustrating.

I take a deep breath, trying not to let my

emotions take over. "Okay, fine. I made a mistake. Maybe I shouldn't have tuned my wand, but it has never misbehaved. At least punish me, not my Grammie. She didn't do anything wrong. Just suspend my wandmaker license, not the shop's."

"Unfortunately, I can't lift the suspension until an inspection has been carried out. And after your confession, I'm afraid I'll have to write you up as well. I apologise, but here at the CWC, we do it by the book, Miss Gemstone."

"What?" Somehow, I've managed to make things worse and not better. At the very least there might be a chance that my confession will help Grammie, but that doesn't solve my current problem.

Before he can explain, the door behind me opens and two buff men in suits step in. They're everything I expect burly security guards to be, so much so that they're bordering on a cliché. I have to wonder why a government body that deals with wand licenses needs guards like that.

"Gentlemen, thank you for coming." Mr Richards rises from behind his desk. "Please confiscate Miss Gemstone's tuned wand."

"What!?" I rise to my feet, horror written all over my face.

He can't be serious. They can't do this to me.

Taking a witch's wand is like taking their finger. Or something else that's vitally important. It's part of me, I can't just be without it.

I snatch my wand from his desk and the whole room tenses. The two men whip out their own wands and point them at me.

"Drop your wand and put your hands on your head where we can see them, Miss Gemstone," the tallest of the security guards commands. "Slowly."

"Slowly!" the other shouts.

Talk about an overreaction, I haven't even done anything to warrant the response.

"No need to treat me like a criminal," I scoff. I briefly contemplate resisting, but that's not going to do Grammie or the shop any good. I have to think about that rather than whether or not I get to leave the room with my wand.

My hands shake as I hold it out to the men.

"Be careful with it," I say needlessly.

"We know what we're doing when it comes to handling wands, Miss Gemstone," Mr Richards says.

I glare at him. Somehow, I doubt he cares about any wand other than his own. Both of his wands.

Damn, I'm too stressed to even laugh at my own wands jokes now.

Reassured I'm no longer a threat, Mr Richards

sits back behind his desk. "You'll be hearing from us soon, Miss Gemstone. Don't leave the area."

I scowl. I'm not a criminal. I shouldn't be treated like one. Instead of pointing that out, I nod. There's nothing I can do right here. It's clear that Mr Richards is no friend of mine. So instead of trying to get him to change my mind, I'm going to be a good little witch and file all of the paperwork I'm supposed to.

No matter what happens, I will get my wand back, and I will get the suspension lifted on Grammie's shop.

CHAPTER FIVE

A witch without a wand is nothing. There's nothing worse than doing dishes by hand. I don't mind doing certain tasks by hand, but the dishes aren't part of that list.

Maybe I'm being dramatic, but I'm feeling a little lost without my wand. It's like my phone to me. I wouldn't want to be without that either.

"Ugh." I dunk my fingers into the scalding hot tea and manage to grab the corner of the teabag. I fling the plump wet bag into the trash and shiver. Gross. I can't wait until my suspension is lifted.

At least the first part of the workshop to sort that out is today. If I ace it, the suspension won't just be lifted, I'll get a sea glass license too. If I fail… I don't even want to think about the consequences for me and the shop. Grammie could lose everything and my punishment would be harsh. When I'm in prison, I'll have different things to worry about than taking out tea bags with my bare hands.

"You brought this upon yourself," Grammie notes as she elegantly removes her tea bag with a flick of her wand. I don't know why she couldn't have done that for mine too. Probably because she's trying to teach me a lesson about going and seeing important people and accidentally revealing my rule-breaking to them. I have to hand it to her, I don't think she's wrong in encouraging me not to do that.

"I was just trying to fix things," I mutter, trying to ignore the guilt. It's not too bad when it's just me who has to suffer, but Grammie is another matter.

No one messes with my Grammie while I'm around. Though maybe in the future I should let her deal with her own problems instead of making them worse.

"And I appreciate the effort, but the CWC isn't to be messed with. The restrictions and rules are there for a reason." She looks at me from over her mug. "Sea glass, Amy? Really? I taught you better than that."

I cast my eyes down. "I'm sorry, Grammie. I didn't see the harm in making slight modifications.

The sea glass really complimented my gemstone and it is stable, no matter what they say."

A smug smile stretches over her face revealing how she really feels about my addition of a second magnifier.

"Of course, you didn't. You're too clever for your own good. And too reckless. You got that from me. But there's a time and a place." The doorbell chimes and Grammie smiles. "On the dot, as expected from the CWC."

With dread weighing down my heart, I follow her from the kitchen down into the shop. Dust is already gathering everywhere and we haven't even suspended for a week. Metaphorical dust, anyway. Grammie would never let the shop get actually dusty.

This is such bullshit. We make the best wands in town, we shouldn't be forced to close. Maybe I should have told the CWC that they were inflicting a travesty on the witches of Yorkshire by making us close our doors.

Grammie unlocks the door and a short woman in a suit smiles politely as she steps inside.

"Morning. Toni of the Riverton Coven, CWC supervisor. I'm here to escort Amethyst of the Gemstone Coven for The Harvest."

I muster a smile. "That's me."

Well, technically it's my Grammie too. One of the many reasons I plan on giving my children unique names that aren't shared with anyone else in the coven.

"Excellent." She reaches inside for a small notebook and clicks her pen demonstratively. "Shall we?" she asks like I have a choice.

"We shall." It's better if I don't fight this and get it all over with. One quick trip to the beach and a bit of wand testing are all I need to be able to put all of this behind me. I can't wait for that.

CHAPTER SIX

I CAN SMELL the beach five minutes before we arrive and despite the company, I relax slightly. The salty air, the cackling seagulls, the wind through my hair are all so familiar that it takes the edge off the tension I'm feeling. There's nothing like a trip to the beach, though it would be better if the CWC woman wasn't here, but if I close my eyes, I can ignore her and pretend someone else is driving. It's not like she's being particularly talkative. She's probably worried that my recklessness will rub off on her and she'll start doing things at work that she isn't supposed to.

I don't have the heart to break it to her that she's either got a free spirit, or she doesn't.

Once we're out of the car and heading down onto

the beach, I rip my shoes off and throw them in my bag. It's a waste of good beach to be wearing them. "Wooo!" My feet sink into the sand and I wiggle my toes, enjoying the way it feels against my skin. I don't think there's anything that can beat this.

"Miss Gemstone. We're here on official CWC business," Toni warns me.

I shrug. "What, and I can't do that on my bare feet?" I'm not hurting anyone by doing this, and she knows it.

With every step, my feet sink deeper into the hot, soft sand. Ah, what a beautiful day. All I need is a nice cold drink and maybe an umbrella for the shade. I can go and wade through the sea and search for shells and sea glass along the waterline. Some of them are perfect for wands, but others are just pretty.

I reach down to my leg for my wand but come up empty. Right, the suspension. Somehow, despite being here with a CWC agent, I already forgot.

With a sigh, I look back, just in time to watch the CWC woman stumble as her shoe disappears into the fluffy sand. She grumbles and I can tell she wishes she hadn't worn socks today. Her mistake. I made it clear in my paperwork that my case would involve heading to the beach.

I skip to the darker part of the beach. The wet sand curls underneath my toes and leaves deep imprints as I wade through shallow pools left behind by the tide. We're not close enough to the sea to find anything interesting yet, but I love how the puddles gradually heat up during the day. It's the second-best part of the beach.

The first…

I race towards the sea and it greets my ankles with a foamy wave. The freezing cold water splashes up against my skin and just as quick as it came, it retreats. The sludgy sand underneath me gurgles and before it can settle, a second wave rolls over my feet.

"We didn't come here to play," Toni shouts from her safe patch of dry sand.

"I'm not playing!" I jump over the next wave and kick the water. "I'm looking." And letting myself be refreshed by nature. I may not belong to one of the sea covens, but sometimes I wonder if there's some of their blood in me anyway. I've always felt at home when surrounded by the sea.

The woman mumbles and grumbles behind me, but I don't care. There's no such thing as hurrying or rushing when it comes to scavenging along the beach. Anyone who says otherwise doesn't understand how the ocean works. The currents will bring what the currents bring. Sometimes, the sea doesn't want me to have anything. Sometimes, I'll return home with bucketfuls of finds.

Another wave rolls over my feet and exposes a couple of broken seashells. I reach down to pick up a black rock and run my thumb over the smooth surface.

"You found a piece already?" the CWC woman asks.

"Don't be silly." I throw the rock back into the water and turn with a big grin. "Finding sea glass takes time. We could be here all day."

"Yippee," she replies sarcastically.

"Do you not like the beach?" I cock my head to the side, realising that she probably doesn't have an affinity for this stuff.

"What's there to like? Too hot, too sandy, and nothing to do."

"That's why it's so great."

"Hmm…"

A pang of pity goes through me as I realise how cruel it is of her superiors to send her if they know how much she dislikes it.

For the first time, I give the woman a good look. Her short hair makes her look less stern than she sounds and the big suit appears as if it's a couple of sizes too big.

"What's your star sign?" I ask.

She blinks a few times, clearly taken aback by my change of subject. "Sorry?"

"I bet you're a Capricorn," I guess. "No, no. Aries. You vibe like one. I knew an Aries. Very friendly girl, always wore her hair in pigtails. And she loved to eat soup. She ate soup every day for lunch, no matter if it was hot or cold. It was just soup, soup, soup. Do you like soup?"

Toni sighs. "Just get on with the search, Miss Gemstone."

"Totally an Aries," I decide.

With my back turned to Toni, I wander along the shoreline, scouring for a glint or a twinkle. Sea glass has a tendency to catch the corner of my eye so it's best not to search too intently.

Every now and then, I bend down to examine something further. A beautiful seashell, a funny-shaped rock, a stray piece of seaweed. There's so much stuff that washes up on the beach every day, I wish I could take it all home but I can't imagine Grammie is in the mood for another shore haul. Sometimes she can be persuaded when I find something useful for wand making. Which only makes me assume that any sea witch blood is from Dad's side of the family, not Mum's.

"Have you found any yet?" Toni questions for the fourth or fifth time. I don't know if she's impatient by nature, or if it's part of the stresses caused by working at the CWC.

"No, not yet."

"You're aware you need ten pieces for the next part of the testing, right?"

"I am aware. Why is it ten pieces? Is there any significance in the number? I think nine sounds better. It's nice and round, three times three. Very pleasing." And magical. Though seven would be that too. But ten? There's nothing special about the number ten.

"I don't know why it's that many," she admits.

I look at the other woman and gesture to the sand. "You know, two sets of eyes are better than one."

"Huh?"

"You should help me look," I suggest. I'm not sure if involving her more will make her less grumpy towards me, but it's worth a try.

"I don't think so."

"Come on. It's fun. And it'll help the time pass

quicker." That reason seems to be one she's more likely to go for.

"I don't do fun."

"That's boring. Everyone needs a bit of fun. Is this a piece?" I pick up a random shell and shrug as I throw it into the water. "Nope. Oops. Guess we'll be here all day."

I can practically hear Toni roll her eyes. "Fine. What am I looking for?"

"Something smooth and colourful and slightly translucent. Brighter than any shell or any rock, almost like a gemstone. You'll know it when you see it." I don't know how to explain better.

Despite her protests, Toni starts looking alongside me. We work in silence for about ten minutes, covering a surprisingly large amount of beach. I kind of like having someone to work alongside. My sister and I used to do it when we were small, before Topaz moved away to be all rebellious and Topazy.

After a while, something catches my eye. I lean down and pick it up, satisfaction and relief crashing through me as I realise it's what we've been looking for.

What was once an ordinary piece of glass has been smoothed out by the never stopping currents, charged by the power of the sea and the moon. There are a thousand colours hidden in this small piece of sea glass, each more beautiful than the other. Just from holding it, I can feel the magic, the potential. It holds pure energy.

I hold it out in my flat hand. "This is sea glass."

"It's pretty," she admits begrudgingly.

"Isn't it? But it's more than that. It's powerful." I'm not sure how I know what sea glass is capable of, but as soon as I put it into my wand I discovered how right I am.

"I'll believe it when I see it," Toni replies.

"Oh, you'll see it."

"Only if you can find nine more pieces before six o'clock."

"What's six o'clock?"

"The end of my workday."

"How boringly rigid." I shrug. "Not you, the CWC. Oh, found another piece." I bend down and pick it up. It isn't as nice as the first piece but it will do. It'll still serve its purpose as a test piece.

Only eight more to go.

"Rover, no!" Someone shouts.

I dismiss it as beach noise until an excitable dog splashes through the water beside me. He looks up with big imploring eyes and a tail wagging a mile-a-minute.

I don't need to be able to speak dog to know what he wants.

"Hello, buddy." I scratch his head, getting an excitable yip from him. His tail goes even faster despite me not even thinking it was possible. "Good boy."

"Rover!"

"I think you have to go back to your owner," I tell him.

Toni clears her throat.

"And I have work to do. Maybe we can play another time?"

He barks happily.

"Rover!"

"Go on, good boy." I point in the direction of the man shouting the dog's name.

Rover jumps to attention, splashing sea water up against me. I smile widely. I love animals. I don't know why we don't have one in the shop. I guess there is Herb, but I'm not sure a gargoyle counts.

"Rover!"

This time the dog responds to his name and bounces off in the direction of his owner.

I sigh wistfully.

"Sea glass," Toni reminds me, pulling me out of my blissful animal haze.

"Yes, I know. We need to find ten pieces by six. We'll have them," I promise her, certain that the sea will deliver. It always does when I need it to, and today is no different.

And once we're done here, I'll be one step closer to removing the suspension from us.

CHAPTER SEVEN

THE CWC WORKSHOP IS HUGE. Massive beams, concrete floors, metalwork tables fit for a medical clinic. They definitely take their wand making seriously.

Despite wand making not being my calling, I can't help but be impressed. And want to work in here. If I could just have a couple of hours alone with some quality materials and all the equipment in this room, I could create something truly amazing. No one would question my capabilities again after that and I'd have all the licenses I wanted.

But that's not how it works. At least I can be certain I'll have a sea glass license by the end of the day. I know how the material behaves as a magnifier, and I'm confident the results won't indicate that it's unstable.

A guard in a hazmat suit escorts me to my workbench where the bag of sea glass is waiting for me. It doesn't look like much but I know these ten pieces are enough to create some excellent wands. I just wish they let me bring my own tools or let me play with the fancier ones dotted around the room. Instead, they've given me access to the standard equipment any wandmaker knows how to use. A couple of chisels to shave down excess wood and shape the wand, a blunt pencil for markings, a bunch of files, a sturdy knife. Nothing out of the ordinary, but I'll still be able to do a good job with them. A big part of the end result depends on the skill of the wandmaker, not the equipment used. Even with poor quality tools I should be able to make a good wand, and these aren't bad, they're just not my preferred brand.

I run my hand over the different woods the CWC has supplied. Three types of regular hardwood. Ash, oak, and maybe maple? I find it interesting that they haven't told me what I'm working with. It's almost as if they're testing more than just the sea glass.

Or they're hoping I don't have the skills to create the pieces they need to test on. They're going to be disappointed if that's the case. I never back down on a challenge, and I do everything in my power not to lose them either.

I lift each of the pieces of wood to my nose and give them each a quick sniff, confirming my suspicions about which of them to choose to make my wands. I set down the wood I plan to use in front of me and put the other two to the side.

The blocks of softwood will be a little more challenging. Pine and fir are delicate and splinter easily. If I'm not careful with those and make them nice and robust, they won't be able to channel the magic without exploding. We can't have that.

The wood I want to use will need some heavy work to shape, but I shouldn't have any trouble with it. I've been making wands like this since Grammie first started to teach me. The two branches and the set of roots will be a much bigger challenge.

I give the roots a little bend. As expected, soft and extremely flexible. Root wands are easy to craft and notoriously difficult to perfect. Since they're mostly used for children as growing wands, most people don't bother putting in the effort to streamline them but somehow, I don't think the CWC will accept anything sub-par. It's the one thing we can agree on. I don't want to either.

Better get to work.

I hum to myself as I begin to whittle down the wood to the right size and shape. I have no idea how my process compares to other wandmakers, I never pay much attention to them when I'm on my training courses. It's not that I try to be unaware of my surroundings, but more because I need to listen to what the wand I'm making wants. It's hard to do that if I'm distracted by anything. Including other people.

Once they're the right size, I start working on the shape. Even though I'm making test wands, I can't help but put in some extra intricacies. The beauty of the sea glass doesn't deserve to be placed into something that isn't as equally wonderful. This part is often what takes the longest, especially when it involves setting the sea glass into place. Everything has to be done by hand when it comes to making wands, using my own would only damage the conductive power of it. But there's still magic that goes into it. I'm not sure how it works, and despite my curious nature, I don't think I want to, either. But when my hands and tools are shaping a wand, I can feel my magic responding to it and giving it the magical strength.

Which is why the wandmaker is more important than the tools.

A couple of hours later, I'm covered in wood shavings and sawdust. My hands are sore from whittling and threatening to blister and the stench of varnish burns my nose as I breathe in. I can't remember the last time I made ten wands in one go. Maybe… never?

Only an idiot or a fool would do this on a regular basis. It's exhausting, both from the physical labour, and the magic needed in order to make them properly.

I wave at one of the guards. "Done!"

He nods without saying anything and two other men with small suitcases join him to collect my precious wands.

"Careful!" I scold as they manhandle my babies.

"Miss Gemstone, we know what we're doing," the tallest guard says, echoing what they said when they removed my wand.

I scowl. Their actions say something completely different from their words.

"Doesn't look like it." I push one of them aside and take over putting the wands in the cases. I've spent all this time crafting them, I'm not going to let them ruin all my hard work.

The guard sighs but lets me do my thing. I'm probably not the first person who insists on doing this. Any wandmaker worth their salt wouldn't be able to stop themselves.

With a satisfying click, I seal the cases and push them to the guards. "There. That's how you pack a wand."

"Hmm." The man gives me a polite smile. "Thank you for your cooperation. You may go now. We'll notify you with the results."

"Okay." I get up from my chair and stretch the tension out of my limbs. Sitting down crouched over my table like a goblin isn't good for my posture. "Is there tea in your waiting room?"

"I think you misunderstand. It will be multiple weeks before we reach a verdict."

"Right… I hope there's enough tea in your waiting room then," I joke.

Nobody smiles.

Pff. Sour plums.

"Orrrr I'll see myself out," I say, doing my best not to roll my eyes. Ugh. Bureaucracy. Again.

CHAPTER EIGHT

EXACTLY THREE WEEKS LATER, I walk through the sliding doors of the CWC with my letter tightly clasped in my fist. Verdict day. I don't know why they couldn't have told me the results via a letter, especially when they seemed perfectly fine with letting us know about our suspension that way. I'll never understand the Centre for Wand Control.

With every step, I have to remind myself to keep breathing and not be too loud. They don't appreciate that here. Or much, to be fair. But that's not the point.

Without looking up from her computer, the same secretary greets me at the front desk. "Morning."

"Good morning." Wow, I even sound nervous. I don't think that's ever happened before.

"What can I do for you?" she asks, seeming oblivious to who I am. I must not have made a big scene after all. Either that or they're used to people reacting that way when they get letters.

I release a tight breath. "I'm here to see Mr Richards."

"Of course." She clicks her mouse a couple of times. "And do you have an—"

"Appointment?" I interrupt. "Abso-freakin-lutely. Amethyst of the Gemstone Coven."

The woman finally looks up at me, her eyes widening with recognition. "Oh, you. Let me check the schedule."

"Sure, sure." I resist the urge to tap; my nails against the smooth surface of the reception desk. I'm sure it will only annoy her.

Her keyboard clatters and she shoots me a surprised smile. "Please take a seat, Miss Gemstone. Mr Richards will be ready for you in five minutes."

"Excellent." Though I wish they'd stop referring to me that way. It must be a modern change to make witches fit in more with some of the other species. But I don't like it. I never thought I was a traditionalist, but it turns out I might be.

I bridge the wait by getting myself a couple of chocolate bars from their vending machine and stuff myself like a stressed panda. I hope my wands passed the tests and they'll lift my suspension. If they don't…

It isn't worth thinking about. I've been training to be a wandmaker since I was fifteen and the Paranormal Police Department already crushed my actual dream of becoming a law enforcement officer. I suppose I could try again, but I doubt they're going to take a witch who failed a CWC evaluation.

I twiddle a piece of string around my thumbs, winding it tight and releasing it when my skin turns white. I do it over and over, jumping at every sound or noise. What's wrong with me? I'm not this person.

A gust of wind draws my attention to the sliding doors as two PPD agents walk in.

Shit.

I hope they're not here to arrest me? What if they are?

No, I won't have failed the test. Even if this is not my passion, I know how to make wands. Grammie taught me and she's the best. Even if people consider sea glass unstable, I know how to use it and how to draw out its powers. Those wands will be the best, most stable wands they've ever had made during an assessment, even if they aren't my best work.

I wonder if they will let me take them back to the

shop with me so I can make them better? I shake my head. I doubt they will. They'll want them to stay within the building so they can test them again if they need to.

I catch one of the agents staring at me and my heart stops. Please don't let them be here for me.

They keep walking and pause at the front desk. The secretary greets them with a smile and directs them to the elevators.

Oof.

I release a tight breath as the two PPD agents step away and leave me be. Maybe I'm being a little paranoid, but I really thought… No, it'll be fine. I'll have aced my workshop for my certification and I'm sure my suspension will be lifted. And even if I haven't, it's not really an issue for the PPD anyway.

With the agents gone, I munch on another chocolate bar until I spot Mr Richards walking in my direction. Guess he doesn't want me in his office then. Not that I blame him after last time. I wait for the guilt over that to come, but it doesn't.

He greets me with a polite smile. "Amethyst of the Gemstone Coven."

Oh good, he's greeting me properly.

"Richard Richards."

His smile turns sour at his full name, but he

manages to keep his professional composure. "It's good to see you again, Miss Gemstone." Ah. So much for that.

"Great. So, what's the result?" I ask, not wasting any time. I'm not here for chit chat and small talk, I want my wand back.

He holds out a translucent folder. "After thorough examination and inspection of the wands you created with sea glass, the CWC came to a conclusion about your suspension and the usage of this magnifier."

Ugh. So much official talk. Why can't he just tell me what I want to know rather than dressing it up in fancy words?

Somehow, I manage to bite my tongue. But it's hard to.

Mr Richards nods reluctantly. "Congratulations, Miss Gemstone. The suspension has been lifted."

"Yes!" I clap my hands together and squeal. "I knew it, I knew it."

"Here's your wand."

I can't stop myself from snatching my wand out of his hand. The past few weeks without it have been awful, and I never want to go through that again if I can help it. Next time, I'll try not to get caught when I do something reckless like add a new magnifier to a wand. I'd say that I won't do it again in general, but I know what I'm like and that's not really an option.

"Thank you, Mr Richards. I really appreciate everything the CWC has done."

He raises an eyebrow as if he doesn't believe me. I don't know why, I'm telling the truth. While we may not see eye to eye on some things, I do appreciate that they came through and did the right thing in the end.

"I hope I won't be seeing you again, Miss Gemstone."

"I hope not either," I reply with a smile. "And now I need to go tell Grammie the good news." And spread it far and wide so the customers can start rolling back into the store.

He gives me another tight-lipped smile before disappearing back towards his office without so much as a goodbye.

But even his slightly rude behaviour isn't going to ruin my good mood. I almost skip out of the CWC building, excited to be able to get back to what's important.

Maybe I can even reapply for the PPD now my wand is regulation again. I don't care how long it takes, one day I'm going to be solving crime for them and the paranormal criminal world won't know what's hit it.

The End

Thank you for reading Glass and Sass, we hope you enjoyed a look into Amy's life! If you want to join her when she finally gets a chance to work with the PPD, you can start the main series with Hexes and Vexes: http://books2read.com/hexesandvexes

CO-WRITTEN BOOKS BY LAURA GREENWOOD & ARIZONA TAPE

The Vampire Detective, co-written with Laura Greenwood (completed paranormal mystery)

1. Fangs For Nothing
2. What The Fangs
3. Fangs For All

Twin Souls Trilogy, co-written with Laura Greenwood (completed paranormal romance)

1. Soulswap (also in audio)
2. Soulshift (also in audio)
3. Soultrade (also in audio)

- Twins Souls Boxed Set (also in audio)

Dragon Soul Series, co-written with Laura Greenwood (paranormal romance)

1. Dragon Destiny
2. Dragon Heart
3. Dragon Outcast (Audiobook Available)

Renegade Dragons, co-written with Laura Greenwood (completed paranormal romance)

1. Fifth Soul (also in audio)
2. Fifth Round (also in audio)
3. Fifth Flame (also in audio)

- Renegade Dragons Boxed Set (also in audio)

ALSO BY LAURA GREENWOOD

denotes a completed series

Books in the Obscure World

- Ashryn Barker* (urban fantasy)
- Grimalkin Academy: Kittens* (paranormal academy)
- Grimalkin Academy: Catacombs* (paranormal academy)
- City Of Blood* (urban fantasy)
- Grimalkin Academy: Stakes* (paranormal academy)
- Supernatural Retrieval Agency (urban fantasy)
- The Black Fan (vampire romance)
- Sabre Woods Academy (paranormal academy)
- Scythe Grove Academy (urban fantasy)
- Carnival Of Blades (urban fantasy)
- The Accidental Cupid (paranormal rom-com)

Books in the Forgotten Gods World

- The Queen of Gods* (mythology romance)
- Forgotten Gods (mythology romance)
- Forgotten Gods: Origins (mythology romance)

The Grimm World

- Grimm Academy* (fairy tale academy)
- Fate Of The Crown* (Arthurian academy)
- Once Upon An Academy Series (fairy tale academy)

Books in the Paranormal Council Universe

- The Paranormal Council Series (paranormal romance)
- The Fae Queen Of Winter Trilogy* (paranormal/fantasy)
- Paranormal Criminal Investigations (urban fantasy mystery)
- MatchMater Paranormal Dating App* (paranormal romance)
- The Necromancer Council (urban fantasy)
- Return Of The Fae* (paranormal post-apocalyptic, complete)

Other Series

- The Apprentice Of Anubis (urban fantasy in an alternate world)
- Beyond The Curse (fantasy fairy tale)
- Untold Tales* (fantasy fairy tale)
- The Dragon Duels (urban fantasy dystopia)
- Rosewood Academy (contemporary upper YA)
- ME* (contemporary romance)
- Seven Wardens*, co-written with Skye MacKinnon (fantasy)
- Tales Of Clan Robbins, co-written with L.A. Boruff (urban fantasy Western)
- The Firehouse Feline*, co-written with Lacey Carter Andersen & L.A. Boruff (urban fantasy romance)

Twin Souls Universe

- Twin Souls*, co-written with Arizona Tape (paranormal romance)
- Dragon Soul*, co-written with Arizona Tape (paranormal romance)
- The Renegade Dragons*, co-written with

Arizona Tape (paranormal romance)
- The Vampire Detective*, co-written with Arizona Tape (urban fantasy mystery)
- Amethyst's Wand Shop Mysteries, co-written with Arizona Tape (urban fantasy)

Mountain Shifters Universe

- Valentine Pride*, co-written with L.A. Boruff (paranormal shifter romance)
- Magic and Metaphysics Academy*, co-written with L.A. Boruff (paranormal academy)

Audiobooks: www.authorlauragreenwood.co.uk/p/audio.html

ABOUT LAURA GREENWOOD

Laura is a USA Today Bestselling Author of paranormal, fantasy, and urban fantasy romance (though she can occasionally be found writing contemporary romance). When she's not writing, she drinks a lot of tea, tries to resist French macarons, and works towards a diploma in Egyptology. She lives in the UK, where most of her books are set.

FOLLOW THE AUTHOR

- Website: www.authorlauragreenwood.co.uk
- Mailing List: www.authorlauragreenwood.co.uk/p/mailing-list-sign-up.html
- Facebook Group: http://facebook.com/groups/theparanormalcouncil
- Facebook Page: http://facebook.com/authorlauragreenwood

- Bookbub: www.bookbub.com/authors/laura-greenwood
- Instagram: www.instagram.com/authorlauragreenwood
- Twitter: www.twitter.com/lauramg_tdir

ALSO BY ARIZONA TAPE

The Samantha Rain Mysteries (urban fantasy f/f)

1. The Case Of The Night Mark
2. The Case Of the Pixie Deal
3. The Case Of The Ruby Curse

- The Case Of The Puppy Academy

The Afterlife Academy: Valkyrie (urban fantasy academy f/f)

1. Valkyrie 101 (also in audio)
2. Valkyrie 102 (also in audio)
3. Valkyrie 103 (also in audio)
4. Valkyrie 104 (also in audio)
5. Valkyrie 105
6. Valkyrie 106
7. Valkyrie 107

- Wings of Grief

The Heir Of The East (completed paranormal academy

f/f

1. Valkyrie's Oath
2. Valkyrie's Choice

My Own Human Duology (completed paranormal dystopian f/f romance)

1. My Own Human
2. Your Own Human

- My Own Human Boxed Set

My Winter Wolf Trilogy (completed paranormal fantasy f/f romance)

1. Wolf's Whisper (also in audio)
2. Wolf's Echo (also in audio)
3. Wolf's Howl
4. A Squad Of Wolves (Danny's Story)

- White Wolf, Black Wolf (Short Story Prequel)
- My Winter Wolf Trilogy Boxed Set

Rainbow Central (new adult f/f romance)

- Love Is For Later
- New Lease Of Love (also in audio)
- Please Be My Love
- Love For The Holidays

The Romance Projects (contemporary)

- Project Crush

Twisted Trilogy (dark contemporary f/f romance)

1. Play To Kiss (also in audio)
2. Play To Kill (also in audio)
3. Play To Keep

Standalone Contemporary Titles

- The Love Pill (f/f) (also in audio)
- Four Gamers and Me (Poly with f/f)
- Choosing Her Boxed Set

Standalone Fantasy

- Beyond the Northern Lights
- Grimm's Dweller

ABOUT ARIZONA TAPE

A creator at heart, Ari has always been in love with the idea of turning nothing into something. She wants to conquer the book world with stories that focus on inclusivity and diversity, writing what she likes to read. Whether it's adventure or romance, dragons and vampires, or princesses and students, there's something for everyone.

FOLLOW THE AUTHOR

- Website: www.arizonatape.com
- Mailing List: www.arizonatape.com/subscribe
- Facebook Page: http://facebook.com/arizonatapeauthor
- Reader Group: http://facebook.com/groups/arizonatape
- Bookbub: http://www.bookbub.com/authors/arizona-tape

- Instagram: http://instagram.com/arizonatape

Ingram Content Group UK Ltd.
Milton Keynes UK
UKHW010820260623
424053UK00004B/266